SIMON & SCHUSTER BOOKS FOR YOUNG READERS

An imprint of Simon & Schuster Children's Publishing Division
1230 Avenue of the Americas, New York, New York 10020
Text copyright © 2000 by Marion Dane Bauer. Illustrations copyright
© 2000 by Pamela Rossi. All rights reserved including the right of
reproduction in whole or in part in any form. SIMON & SCHUSTER
BOOKS FOR YOUNG READERS is a trademark of Simon & Schuster.
Book design by Paul Zakris. The text for this book is set in 18-point
Horley Old Style Medium. The illustrations are rendered in pastel.
Printed in Hong Kong
10 9 8 7 6 5 4 3 2 1

LIBRARY OF CONGRESS CATALOGING-IN-PUBLICATION DATA

Bauer, Marion Dane.
Grandmother's song / by Marion Dane Bauer ; illustrated by Pamela
Rossi.
    p.   cm.
Summary: A woman celebrates the arrival of her baby girl and then,
years later, the similar arrival of her grandson.
ISBN 0-689-82272-3
[1. Babies—Fiction. 2. Mother and child—Fiction.
3. Grandmothers—Fiction.] I. Rossi, Pamela, ill. II. Title.
PZ7.B3262Gr 2000
[E]—dc21
98-31658

# Grandmother's Song

by Marion Dane Bauer

illustrated by Pamela Rossi

Simon & Schuster Books for Young Readers

NEW YORK   LONDON   TORONTO   SYDNEY   SINGAPORE

For my daughter, Beth-Alison,
and my grandson, Barrett Christopher
—*M. D. B.*

To Anne, Maria, and Eleanor,
in honor of all my ancestors
—*P. R.*

*Long ago,* when rain was wet
  and the moon waxed and waned,
long, long ago, when kittens were soft
  and fish flashed, silver quick, in the water . . .
all that long ago, a baby lay curled inside my belly.

She bloomed inside me like a loaf of bread,
   rising, rising.
She sprouted like a mushroom
   in the secret dark.
She grew and my belly grew
   until I thought I might burst.

Then she pushed, pushed,
into the air,
into the light,
into my arms.

I held her.

I rocked her.

I counted her fingers
   and kissed her nose.

I licked her toes and
   traced the shape of her chin.

And I sang, "My daughter,
my daughter, daughter, daughter,
welcome.
Welcome to the world."

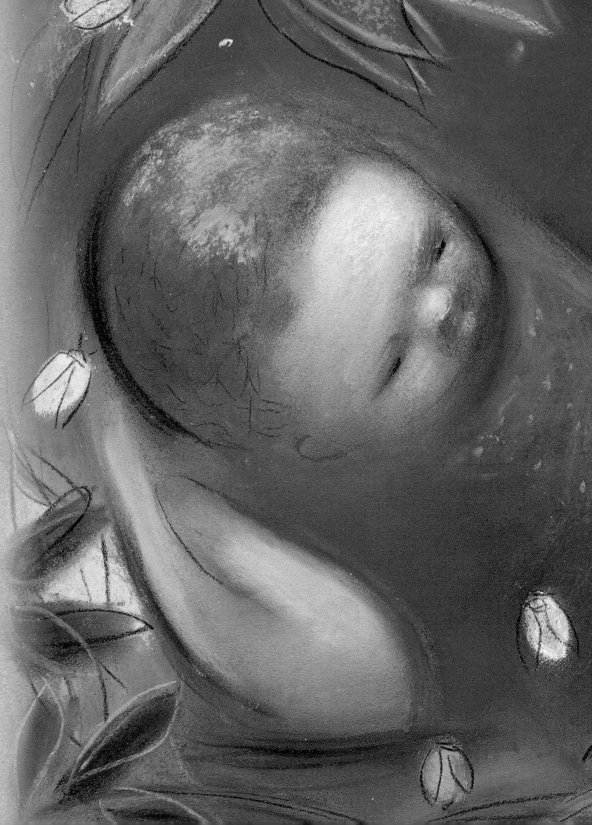

She smiled at me, and she began to grow.

She grew until she crawled.

She grew until she walked.

She grew until she ran

and leapt

and danced.

And sometimes tumbled down.

Then ran
and leapt
and danced again.
She grew into a woman.

Then,

not so long ago, when snow was cold

   and grass grew green,

a little while ago, when elephants were large

   and hives dripped honey,

just that short time ago,

   a baby grew inside her belly,

a baby grew inside my heart.

He bloomed like fragrant bread
   filling an oven.
He sprouted like a mushroom where
   mushrooms had only been dreamed before.
He grew,
and my daughter's belly grew,
and my heart grew until we both
   thought we might burst.

Then he pushed, pushed,
into the air,
into the light,
into our arms.

We held him.

We rocked him.

We counted his fingers
    and kissed his nose.

We licked his toes and
    traced the shape of his chin.

And I sang, "My grandson,
my grandson, grandson,
    grandson,
welcome.
Welcome to the world."

Rain and moon, kittens and fish,
    snow and grass, elephants and honey,
I give them to you.